FRANKENSTEIN

Adapted & Illustrated by

CHRIS MOULD

OXFORD UNIVERSITY PRESS

CAPTAIN WALTON'S DIARY

My crew were hearty and loyal. They could keep themselves amused and their patience was beyond the limits of my own.

Time stood still while we were trapped on the ice. We heard and saw nothing. Only the passing of day and night could ensure that we were still upon this earth. My mind had taken me on many a journey but still I returned to this limbo, locked in until the thaw came.

Our boredom was broken one evening by a voice shouting from the top of the mast. As I reached the deck I viewed a figure drifting towards us on the ice. We pulled his wasted body aboard and he whispered his name . . . 'Victor . . . Victor Frankenstein.'

We took him to my cabin and when he had recovered he told me his strange and harrowing story.

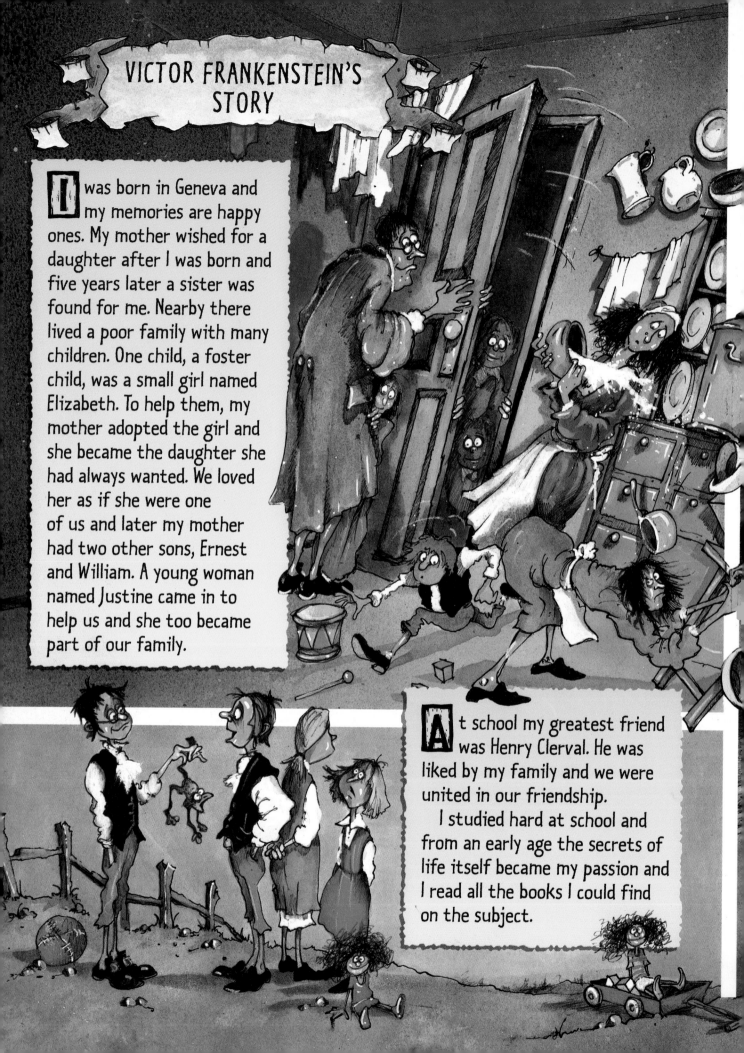

VICTOR FRANKENSTEIN'S STORY

I was born in Geneva and my memories are happy ones. My mother wished for a daughter after I was born and five years later a sister was found for me. Nearby there lived a poor family with many children. One child, a foster child, was a small girl named Elizabeth. To help them, my mother adopted the girl and she became the daughter she had always wanted. We loved her as if she were one of us and later my mother had two other sons, Ernest and William. A young woman named Justine came in to help us and she too became part of our family.

At school my greatest friend was Henry Clerval. He was liked by my family and we were united in our friendship.

I studied hard at school and from an early age the secrets of life itself became my passion and I read all the books I could find on the subject.

When I was fifteen I observed a most violent storm. Before my eyes I saw a huge tree reduced to nothing with a bolt of lightning. Now I knew the power of electricity and I longed to hold its secret in my hands. I abandoned my pursuit of nature and threw myself into studying the new science of galvanism.

For seventeen years I saw only happiness. But then, my mother became ill. We knew that shortly she would die and it was her last wish that one day, Elizabeth and I would be married.

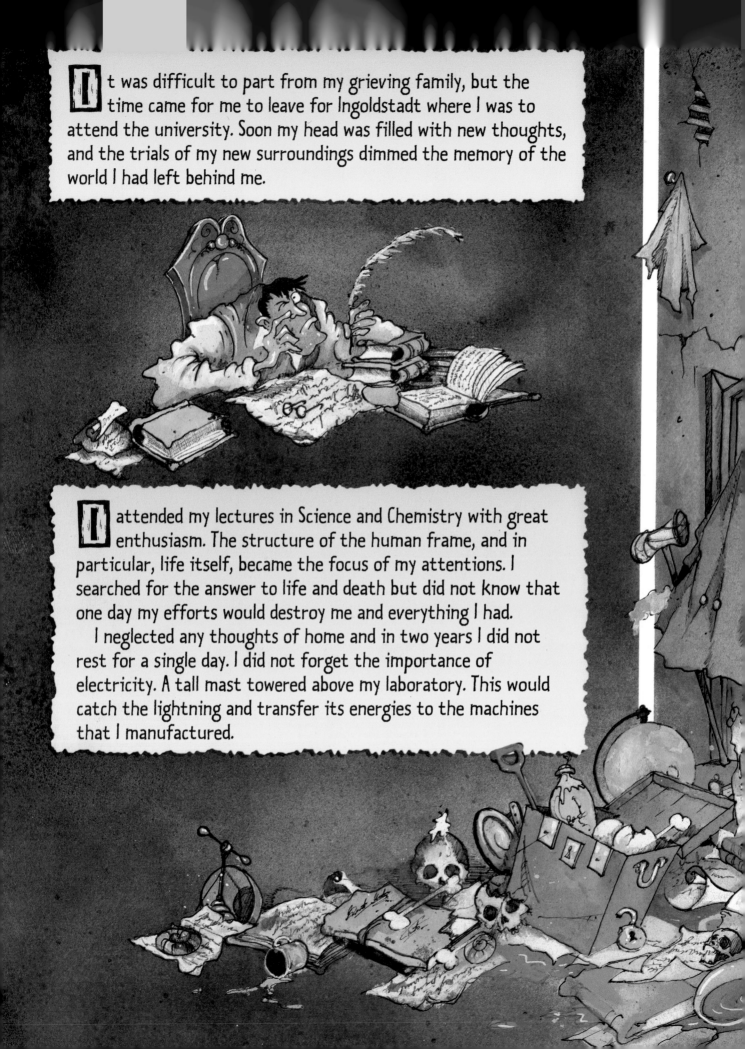

It was difficult to part from my grieving family, but the time came for me to leave for Ingoldstadt where I was to attend the university. Soon my head was filled with new thoughts, and the trials of my new surroundings dimmed the memory of the world I had left behind me.

I attended my lectures in Science and Chemistry with great enthusiasm. The structure of the human frame, and in particular, life itself, became the focus of my attentions. I searched for the answer to life and death but did not know that one day my efforts would destroy me and everything I had.

I neglected any thoughts of home and in two years I did not rest for a single day. I did not forget the importance of electricity. A tall mast towered above my laboratory. This would catch the lightning and transfer its energies to the machines that I manufactured.

My mind was filled with my obsession. I could think of nothing else—except the creation of a human being. And so I began my work.

The seasons passed unnoticed outside my window. I grew weak in the neglect of my own self. At times I caught my reflection, yet I did not recognize the man I saw.

At night I preyed upon tombs and graveyards to gather the grisly materials I needed. A frantic impulse urged me forward. I found myself sickened by my work, yet I continued in my pursuit.

It was on a stormy November night that my work drew to a close. I worked till the early hours of the morning as I tried to inject a spark of life into my creation. My candle was almost burnt out when, to my astonishment, I saw the eye of the creature open. It lived.

Suddenly the beauty of my dream vanished. I saw the monster I had created and at last I came to my senses. Unable to even look at the creature, I left the room, securing the lock. For hours I wandered the apartment, breathless in horror, trying to compose myself. At last I lay on my bed, exhausted. I slept badly and when I awoke, there was the creature looming over me.

Before its huge hand touched me I was gone, into the courtyard where I stayed until morning.

I wandered the town in a daze and did not notice a train arriving from Geneva. Someone ran towards me. It was my good friend Henry Clerval. He shook my hand warmly, smiling as he spoke. 'How glad I am to see you. I have only good news.

Your family are all well and I am to join you at the university.'

In his happiness he did not notice my fragile state. I was delighted to see Henry again and forgot my fears. But when we reached my house, I asked him to wait outside in case the monster was waiting.

But he had gone. I pushed away all thoughts of the creature and soon we were laughing and joking. Suddenly Henry cried, 'My dear Victor, are you ill?'

Before I could answer I fell to the floor in a fit. When I came round, Henry was at my side. For two months he nursed me day and night.

One morning a letter arrived from my father. The news was terrible. My brother William had been murdered. At once we left for Geneva and as we rode into town I swear I saw the beast I had created. Could he have murdered my poor brother? I could not doubt it.

The joy of being reunited with my family was smothered by grief.

'We were out walking,' said my father, 'and the children were playing hide and seek. William had hidden from Ernest and before long he was missing. I found him at five o'clock the next morning. He had worn a chain around his neck with a picture of your mother. We think someone murdered him to steal the chain.'

Soon it was announced that the chain had been found in Justine's pocket. She was arrested.

We all knew Justine was not capable of this atrocity. Only I knew the real truth, yet who would believe me?

We were sure that Justine would be free after the trial, but we were wrong. She was found guilty and she was sent away to a darkened cell where she waited quietly for her death. She would die because of me, William had died because of me. I saw the decay that ate at my family and knew that I was the cause.

I became ill again and even Elizabeth's love could not help me. I walked alone for days and days—into the Alps, among the mountains where the peace and tranquillity swallowed me whole. One morning I saw a figure heading towards me. Moving fast, it jumped over rocks and crevices. Soon I could see it was the monster I had created.

'You are evil!' I cried. 'You have killed those I love!'

'Your unhappiness, though deep, does not equal mine,' he replied. 'William and Justine died because you could not show me love. There is something you must do. Come with me and I will tell you my story.'

We sat by a burning fire and he began.

THE CREATURE'S STORY

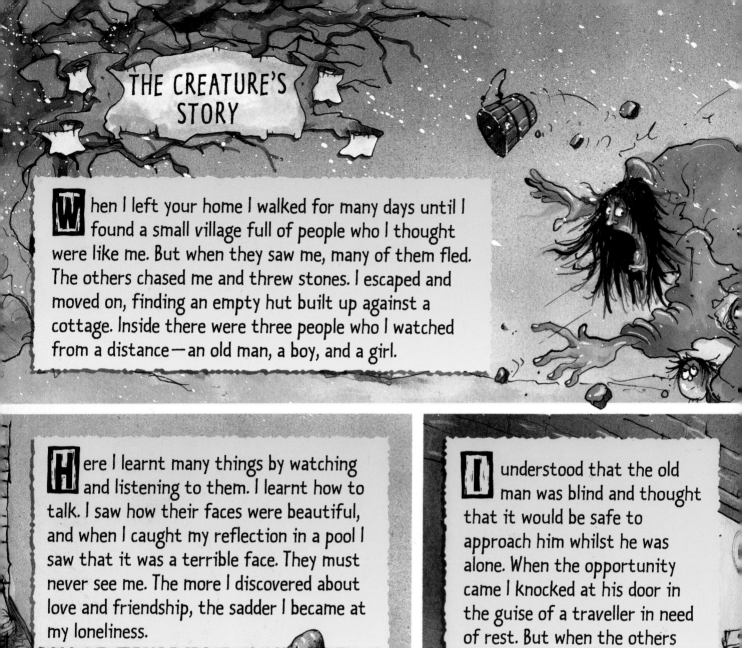

When I left your home I walked for many days until I found a small village full of people who I thought were like me. But when they saw me, many of them fled. The others chased me and threw stones. I escaped and moved on, finding an empty hut built up against a cottage. Inside there were three people who I watched from a distance—an old man, a boy, and a girl.

Here I learnt many things by watching and listening to them. I learnt how to talk. I saw how their faces were beautiful, and when I caught my reflection in a pool I saw that it was a terrible face. They must never see me. The more I discovered about love and friendship, the sadder I became at my loneliness.

I understood that the old man was blind and thought that it would be safe to approach him whilst he was alone. When the opportunity came I knocked at his door in the guise of a traveller in need of rest. But when the others returned they recoiled in horror at the sight of me and the boy beat me to the ground with a stick. I escaped and left.

wo months later I came to Geneva. I slept heavily that night, woken only by a boy who ran into my hiding place. When he saw me he screamed, and in my clumsy attempt to silence him I broke his neck and he lay at my feet. I took a chain from around his neck and left, only to stumble across a young girl sleeping. I put the chain into her pocket and I knew the police would think that she had killed the boy.

And now I am alone and miserable. You must make me a partner like myself and then I will trouble you no more. That much you owe me.

FRANKENSTEIN CONTINUES HIS STORY

I thought long and hard and though I hated the very thought of it I gave my word.

'You must promise me that after this you will disappear for ever.'

He agreed and then he turned and left.

At once I returned to Geneva. I found my family concerned at my distraction and though Elizabeth begged me to stay I left for England where I was to begin my work. I promised her we would marry on my return and at that she was happy. Henry travelled with me at my father's request and later I moved on to Scotland.

Continuing my experiments, I began to feel a great remorse at my actions. One night as I worked, I looked out through my window. There he stood, watching my every move. A sudden anger overwhelmed me and I threw down my tools, abandoning my new creation.

The beast roared in anger. 'I will be with you on your wedding night,' he shouted, and he disappeared through the fog. I took a boat out on to the loch and disposed of all traces of my work.

The following morning held a dreadful shock. The police arrived at my door to arrest me after a murder the previous night. I had been noted as new in the area and my actions were seen as suspicious. They took me along to see the body and to my horror I saw that it was my dear friend Henry Clerval. The monster had struck again. I was thrown into a cell to await my trial and again I was overcome by illness.

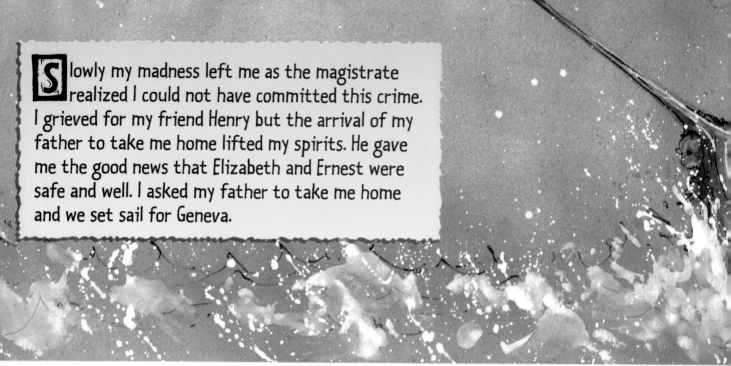

lowly my madness left me as the magistrate realized I could not have committed this crime. I grieved for my friend Henry but the arrival of my father to take me home lifted my spirits. He gave me the good news that Elizabeth and Ernest were safe and well. I asked my father to take me home and we set sail for Geneva.

hen we arrived in Geneva Elizabeth was there to meet me. How I had missed her. I longed to tell my story but how could she ever believe me?

We arranged our wedding but I feared for our lives as I remembered the words of the monster. From that day on I kept a gun closely by my side.

After the wedding Elizabeth and I said goodbye to our guests and left for our honeymoon. We stopped at a peaceful hotel and for the first time for months I felt happy.

In the evening I told Elizabeth to go to bed and I went in search of the monster. As I stood outside, a dreadful scream filled the air.

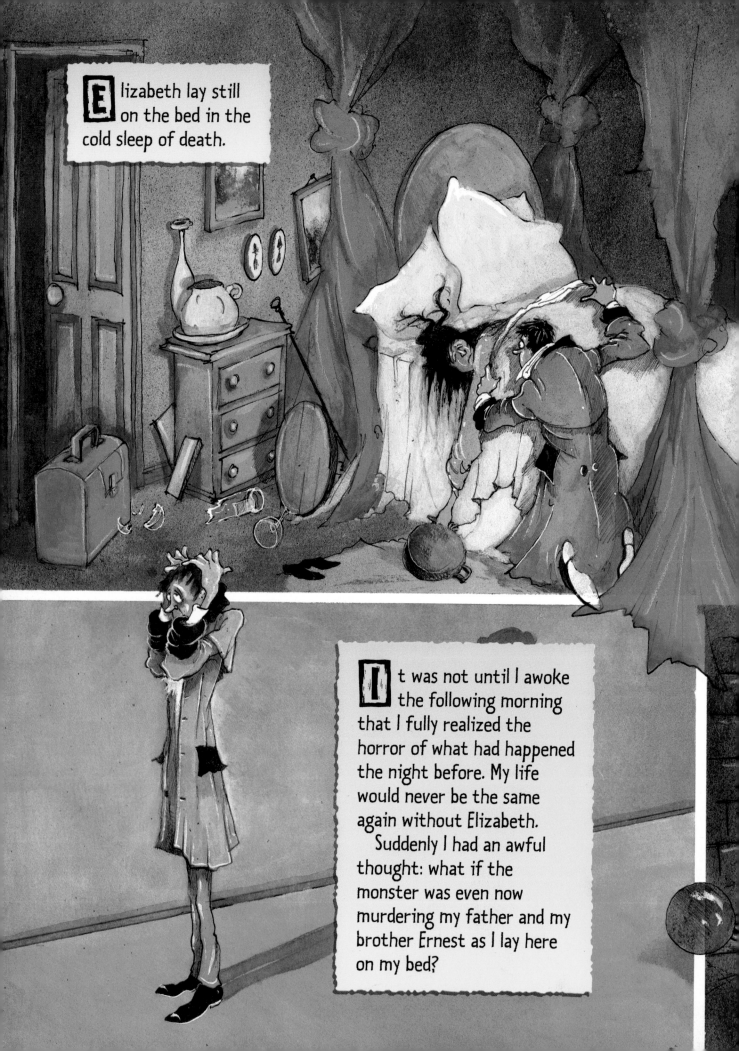

Elizabeth lay still on the bed in the cold sleep of death.

It was not until I awoke the following morning that I fully realized the horror of what had happened the night before. My life would never be the same again without Elizabeth.

Suddenly I had an awful thought: what if the monster was even now murdering my father and my brother Ernest as I lay here on my bed?

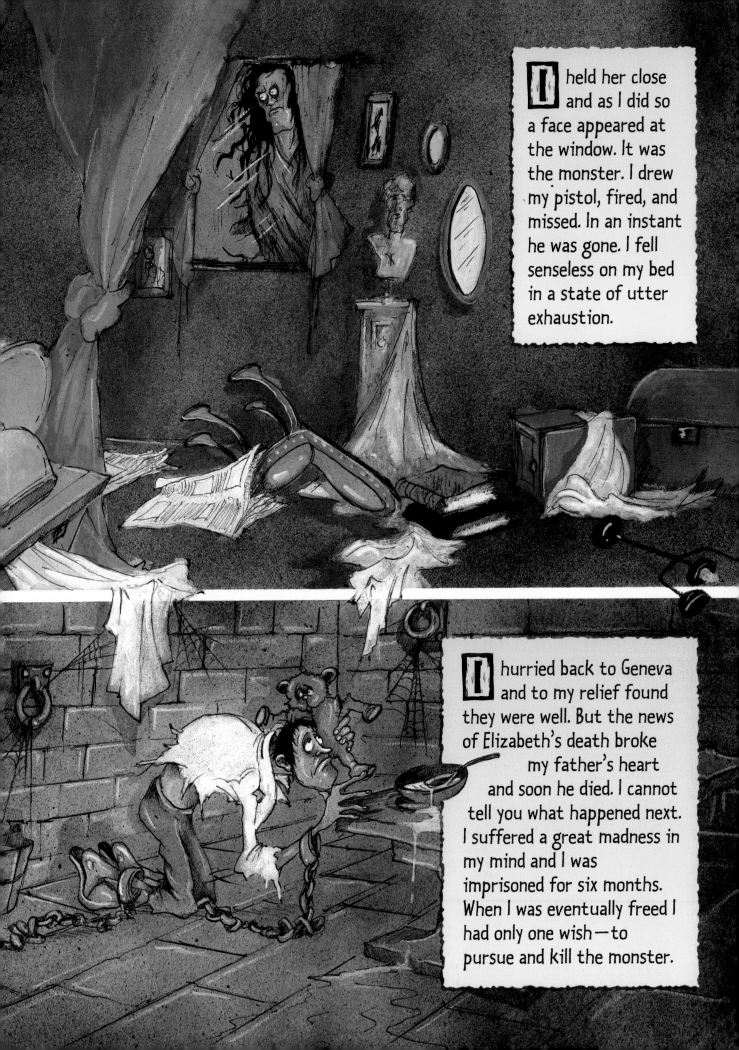

I held her close and as I did so a face appeared at the window. It was the monster. I drew my pistol, fired, and missed. In an instant he was gone. I fell senseless on my bed in a state of utter exhaustion.

I hurried back to Geneva and to my relief found they were well. But the news of Elizabeth's death broke my father's heart and soon he died. I cannot tell you what happened next. I suffered a great madness in my mind and I was imprisoned for six months. When I was eventually freed I had only one wish—to pursue and kill the monster.

I decided to leave Geneva for ever. I knew the monster would head north to the ice where I would feel the misery of cold and frost, but he would not. Often I heard his voice beckoning me. He knew I would pursue him.

Only when I slept was I happy. I dreamed of Elizabeth and my family. Also of my good friend Henry. Soon I would be with them all in my death, but first another life must end.

felt pain from the cold and ice. I was losing hope and then, in the distance, a shape familiar to me moved across the white plain. It was my creation. As I got closer the ice broke and he was carried away by the sea.

drifted along on a piece of ice that grew smaller and smaller until I was sure I would drown. It was then that I saw your ship.

That is my story. I know I have not long to live but I do not fear death. I ask you to kill this monster. Do not speak with him. He can reason as well as any man. There is no more I can say except, I thank you.

CAPTAIN WALTON'S FINAL NOTE

So now you know Victor Frankenstein's story. Poor Victor. He worked so hard to achieve something that in the end he lost everything he had. He died only a few minutes after he had finished his story. Now he would feel his pain no more. The ice was breaking and soon we would be moving on.

We laid his body in a cabin and later I heard a voice from in there. Inside, a large creature stood weeping over Victor's body. He held him close. 'So, I have killed you too,' he said. 'Forgive me.'

'It is too late,' I said. 'He is gone now. You have done enough.'

'Understand one thing,' he cried, 'I have suffered more than anyone. I was shunned by the one who created me. My heart, like yours, was made for love, but no one would let me love. I hate myself more than anyone hates me and now my own death is near.'

I shall go north across the ice and build a great fire. There, I will lie down and die. When the last flame has flickered out, I will be at peace.'

The monster sprang from the window and clambered on to the ice as he said his last words.

The sea carried him away and he was lost in the darkness.